Defoe Abbott Marx Hardy Melville Machiavelli Montaigne Emerson Chesterton Cooper Joyce Austen Hugo Eliot Grimm
Stoker Carroll Christie Haggard Molière
Wilde Maupassant Byron Schiller
Garnett Einstein Fitzgerald Engels Hawthorne Smith Kafka
Goethe Dostoyevsky Hall
Baum Cotton Kipling Doyle Willis
Henry Nietzsche
Leslie Dumas Flaubert Turgenev Balzac
Stockton Vatsyayana Crane
Burroughs Verne
Curtis Tocqueville Gogol Vinci
Homer Widger Tolstoy Whitman Busch
Darwin Thoreau Twain Scott
Potter Freud Zola Lawrence Plato Harte
Kant Jowett Stevenson Dickens Hesse
Andersen Burton
London Descartes Cervantes Cooke
Poe Aristotle Wells Voltaire
Hale James Hastings
Bunner Shakespeare Irving
Richter Chambers
Doré Dante Chekhov da Shaw Benedict Alcott
Swift Wodehouse Pushkin
Newton

 tredition®

tredition was established in 2006 by Sandra Latusseck and Soenke Schulz. Based in Hamburg, Germany, tredition offers publishing solutions to authors and publishing houses, combined with world-wide distribution of printed and digital book content. tredition is uniquely positioned to enable authors and publishing houses to create books on their own terms and without conventional manufacturing risks.

For more information please visit: www.tredition.com

TREDITION CLASSICS

This book is part of the TREDITION CLASSICS series. The creators of this series are united by passion for literature and driven by the intention of making all public domain books available in printed format again - worldwide. Most TREDITION CLASSICS titles have been out of print and off the bookstore shelves for decades. At tredition we believe that a great book never goes out of style and that its value is eternal. Several mostly non-profit literature projects provide content to tredition. To support their good work, tredition donates a portion of the proceeds from each sold copy. As a reader of a TREDITION CLASSICS book, you support our mission to save many of the amazing works of world literature from oblivion. See all available books at www.tredition.com.

Project Gutenberg

The content for this book has been graciously provided by Project Gutenberg. Project Gutenberg is a non-profit organization founded by Michael Hart in 1971 at the University of Illinois. The mission of Project Gutenberg is simple: To encourage the creation and distribution of eBooks. Project Gutenberg is the first and largest collection of public domain eBooks.

The Uses of Astronomy An Oration Delivered at Albany on the 28th of July, 1856

Edward Everett

Imprint

This book is part of TREDITION CLASSICS

Author: Edward Everett
Cover design: Buchgut, Berlin – Germany

Publisher: tredition GmbH, Hamburg - Germany
ISBN: 978-3-8424-8073-5

www.tredition.com
www.tredition.de

CONTENTS

A NOTE EXPLANATORY.

The undersigned ventures to put forth this report of Mr. Everett's Oration, in connection with a condensed account of the Inauguration of the Dudley Observatory, and the Dedication of the New State Geological Hall, at Albany,—in the hope that the demand which has exhausted the newspaper editions, may exhaust this as speedily as possible; not that he is particularly tenacious of a reward for his own slight labors, but because he believes that the extensive circulation of the record of the two events so interesting and important to the cause of Science will exercise a beneficial influence upon the public mind. The effort of the distinguished Statesman who has invested Astronomy with new beauties, is the latest and one of the most brilliant of his compositions, and is already wholly out of print, though scarcely a month has elapsed since the date of its delivery. The account of the proceedings at Albany during the Ceremonies of Inauguration is necessarily brief, but accurate, and is respectfully submitted to the consideration of the reader.

A. MAVERICK.

New York, *October 1, 1856.*

TWO NEW INSTITUTIONS OF SCIENCE;

AND

THE SCENES WHICH ATTENDED THEIR CHRISTENING.

In the month of August last, two events took place in the city of Albany, which have more than an ephemeral interest. They occurred in close connection with the proceedings of a Scientific Convention, and the memory of them deserves to be cherished as a recollection of the easy way in which Science may be popularized and be rendered so generally acceptable that the people will cry, like Oliver Twist, for more. It is the purpose of this small publication to embody, in a form more durable than that of the daily newspaper, the record of proceedings which have so near a relation to the progress of scientific research. A marked feature in the ceremonies was the magnificent Oration of the Hon. Edward Everett, inaugurating the Dudley Observatory of Albany; and it is believed that the reissue of that speech in its present form will be acceptable to the admirers of that distinguished gentleman, not less than to the lovers of Science, who hung with delight upon his words.

THE DEDICATION OF THE GEOLOGICAL HALL.

On Wednesday, August 27, 1856, the State Geological Hall of New York was dedicated with appropriate ceremonies. For the purpose of affording accommodation to the immense crowds of people who, it was confidently anticipated, would throng to this demonstration and that of the succeeding day, at which Mr. Everett spoke, a capacious Tent was arranged with care in the center of Academy Park, on Capitol Hill; and under its shelter the ceremonies of the inauguration of both institutions were conducted without accident or confusion; attended on the first day by fully three thousand persons, and on the second by a number which may be safely computed at from five to seven thousand.

The announcement that Hon. Wm. H. Seward would be present at the dedication of the Geological Hall, excited great interest among the citizens; but the hope of his appearance proved fallacious. His place was occupied by seven picked men of the American

Association for the Advancement of Science, one of whom (Prof. Henry) declared his inability to compute the problem why seven men of science were to be considered equal to one statesman. The result justified the selections of the committee, and although the Senator was not present, [4]the seven Commoners of Science made the occasion a most notable one by the flow of wit, elegance of phrase, solidity and cogency of argument, and rare discernment of natural truths, with which their discourse was garnished.

The members of the American Association marched in procession to the Tent, from their place of meeting in the State Capitol. On the stage were assembled many distinguished gentlemen, and in the audience were hundreds of ladies. Gov. Clark and Ex-Governors Hunt and Seymour, of New York, Sir Wm. Logan, of Canada, Hon. George Bancroft, and others as well known as these, were among the number present. The tent was profusely decorated. Small banners in tri-color were distributed over the entire area covered by the stage, and adorned the wings. The following inscriptions were placed over the front of the rostrum, — that in honor of *The Press* occupying a central position:

GEOLOGY.   THE PRESS.

METEOROLOGY.   MINERALOGY.

METALLURGY.   ETHNOLOGY.

            ASTRONOMY.

The following were arranged in various positions on the right and left:

CHEMISTRY.   TELEGRAPH.

PHYSIOLOGY.

CONCHOLOGY.

PALÆONTOLOGY.

MICROSCOPY.

ART.

STEAM.

COMMERCE.

SCIENCE.

NAVIGATION.

LETTERS.

HYDROLOGY.

ZOOLOGY.

ICHTHYOLOGY.

MANUFACTURES.

AGRICULTURE.

PHYSICS.

ANATOMY.

BOTANY.

The proceedings of the day were opened with prayer by Rev. Geo. W. Bethune, D.D., of Brooklyn.

Hon. Garrit Y. Lansing, of Albany, then introduced Professor Louis Agassiz, of Cambridge, Mass., who was the first of the "seven men of science" to entertain his audience, always with the aid of the inevitable black-board, without which the excellent Professor would be as much at a loss as a chemist without a laboratory. Professor Agassiz spoke for an hour, giving his views of a new theory of animal development. He began by saying:—

We are here to inaugurate the Geological Hall, which has grown out of the geological survey of the State. To make the occasion memorable, a distinguished statesman of your own State, and Mr. Frank C. Gray, were expected to be present and address you. The pressure of public duties has detained Mr. Seward, and severe sickness has detained Mr. Gray. I deeply lament that the occasion is lost to you to hear my friend Mr. Gray, who is a devotee to science, and as warm-hearted a friend as ever I knew. Night before last I was requested to assist in taking their place—I, who am the most unfit of men for the post. I never made a speech. I have addressed learned bodies, but I lack that liberty of speech—the ability to present in finished style, and with that rich imagery which characterize the words of the orator, the thoughts fitting to such an occasion as this. He would limit himself, he continued, to presenting some motives [5]why the community should patronize science, and foster such institutions as this. We scientific men regard this as an occasion of the highest interest, and thus do not hesitate to give the sanction of the highest learned body of the country as an indorsement of the liberality of this State. The geological survey of New York has given to the world a new nomenclature. No geologist can, hereafter, describe the several strata of the earth without referring to it. Its results, as recorded in your published volumes, are treasured in the most valuable libraries of the world. They have made this city famous; and now, when the scientific geologist lands on your shore, his first question is, "Which is the way to Albany? I want to see your fossils." But Paleontology is only one branch of the subject, and many others your survey has equally fostered.

He next proceeded to show that organized beings were organized with reference to a plan, which the relations between different animals, and between different plants, and between animals and plants, everywhere exhibit;—drew sections of the body of a fish, and of the bird, and of man, and pointed out that in each there was the same central back-bone, the cavity above and the ribbed cavity below the flesh on each side, and the skin over all—showing that the maker of each possessed the same thought—followed the same plan of structure. And upon that plan He had made all the kinds of quadrupeds, 2,000 in number, all the kinds of birds, 7,000 in number, all of the reptiles, 2,000 to 3,000 in number, all the fish, 10,000 to 12,000 in number. All their forms may be derived as different expressions of the same formula. There are only four of these great types; or, said he, may I not call them the four tunes on which Divinity has played the harmonies that have peopled, in living and beautiful reality, the whole world?

PROFESSOR HITCHCOCK ON REMINISCENCES.

Erastus C. Benedict, Esq. of New York, introduced Prof. Hitchcock, of Amherst, as a gentleman whose name was very familiar, who had laid aside, voluntarily, the charge of one of the largest colleges in New England, but who could never lay aside the honors he had earned in the literature and science of geology.

After a few introductory observations, Prof. Hitchcock said: —

This, I believe, is the first example in which a State Government in our country has erected a museum for the exhibition of its natural resources, its mineral and rock, its plants and animals, living and fossil. And this seems to me the most appropriate spot in the country for placing the first geological hall erected by the Government; for the County of Albany was the district where the first geological survey was undertaken, on this side of the Atlantic, and, perhaps, the world. This was in 1820, and ordered by that eminent philanthropist, Stephen Van Rensselaer, who, three years later, appointed Prof. Eaton to survey, in like manner, the whole region traversed by the Erie Canal. This was the commencement of a work, which, during the last thirty years, has had a wonderful expansion, reaching a large part of the States of the Union, as well as Canada, Nova Scotia, and New Brunswick, and, I might add, several European countries, where the magnificent surveys now in progress did not commence till after the survey of Albany and Rensselaer Counties. How glad are we, therefore, to find on this spot the first Museum of Economical Geology on this side of the Atlantic! Nay, embracing as it does all the department of Natural History, I see in it more than a European Museum of Economical Geology, splendid though they are. I fancy, rather, that I see here the germ of a Cis-Atlantic British Museum, or Garden of Plants.

North Carolina was the first State that ordered a geological survey; and I have the pleasure of seeing before me the gentleman who executed it, and in 1824-5 published a report of 140 pages. I refer to Professor Olmstead, who, though he has since won brighter laurels in another department of science, will always be honored as the first commissioned State geologist in our land.

[6]

Of the New York State Survey he said: —

This survey has developed the older fossiliferous rocks, with a fullness and distinctness unknown elsewhere. Hence European savans study the New York Reports with eagerness. In 1850, as I entered the Woodwardian Museum, in the University of Cambridge, in England, I found Professor McCoy busy with a collection of Silurian fossils before him, which he was studying with Hall's first volume of Paleontology as his guide; and in the splendid volumes, entitled *British Paleozoric Rocks and Fossils*, which appeared last year as the result of those researches, I find Professor Hall denominated the great American Paleontologist. I tell you, Sir, that this survey has given New York a reputation throughout the learned world, of which she may well be proud. Am I told that it will, probably, cost half a million? Very well. The larger the sum, the higher will be the reputation of New York for liberality; and what other half million expended in our country, has developed so many new facts or thrown so much light upon the history of the globe, or won so world-wide and enviable a reputation?

And of Geological Surveys in general: —

In regard to this matter of geological surveys, I can hardly avoid making a suggestion here. So large a portion of our country has now been examined, more or less thoroughly, by the several State governments, that it does seem to me the time has come when the National government should order a survey — geological, zoological, and botanical — of the whole country, on such a liberal and thorough plan as the surveys in Great Britain are now conducted; in the latter country it being understood that at least thirty years will be occupied in the work. Could not the distinguished New York statesman who was to have addressed us to-day be induced, when the present great struggle in which he is engaged shall have been brought to a close, by a merciful Providence, to introduce this subject, and urge it upon Congress? And would it not be appropriate for the American Association for the Advancement of Science to throw a petition before the government for such an object? Or might it not, with the consent of the eminent gentleman who has charge of the Coast Survey, be connected therewith, as it is with the Ordnance Survey in Great Britain.

The history of the American Association was then given: —

Prof. Mather, I believe, through Prof. Emmons, first suggested to the New-York Board of Geologists in November, 1838, in a letter proposing a number of points for their consideration. I quote from him the following paragraph relating to the meeting. As to the credit he has here given me of having personally suggested the subject, I can say only that I had been in the habit for several years of making this meeting of scientific men a sort of hobby in my correspondence with such. Whether others did the same, I did not then, and do not now know. Were this the proper place, I could go more into detail on this point; but I will merely quote Prof. Mather's language to the Board: —

* * * * "Would it not be well to suggest the propriety of a meeting of Geologists and other scientific men of our country at some central point next fall, — say at New-York or Philadelphia? There are many questions in our Geology that will receive new light from friendly discussion and the combined observations of various individuals who have noted them in different parts of our country. Such a meeting has been suggested by Prof. Hitchcock; and to me it seems desirable. It would undoubtedly be an advantage not only to science but to the several surveys that are now in progress and that may in future be authorized. It would tend to make known our scientific men to each other personally, give them more confidence in each other, and cause them to concentrate their observation on those questions that are of interest in either a scientific or economical point of view. More questions may be satisfactorily [7]settled in a day by oral discussion in such a body, than a year by writing and publication."[A]

[A] In the letter alluded to, on examination, we discover another passage bearing on the point, which, owing to the Professor's modesty we suspect, he did not read. Prof. Mather adds. "You, so far as I know, first suggested the matter of such an Association. I laid the matter before the Board of Geologists of New-York, specifying some of the advantages that might be expected to result; and Prof. Vanuxem probably made the motion before the Board in regard to it."

Though the Board adopted the plan of a meeting, various causes delayed the first over till April, 1840, when we assembled in Philadelphia, and spent a week in most profitable and pleasant discussion, and the presentation of papers. Our number that year was only 18, because confined almost exclusively to the State geologists;

but the next year, when we met again in Philadelphia, and a more extended invitation was given, about eighty were present; and the members have been increasing to the present time. But, in fact, those first two meetings proved the type, in all things essential, of all that have followed. The principal changes have been those of expansion and the consequent introduction of many other branches of science with their eminent cultivators. In 1842, we changed the name to that of the Association of American Geologists and Naturalists; and in 1847, to that of the American Association for the Advancement of Science. I trust it has not yet reached its fullest development, as our country and its scientific men multiply, and new fields of discovery open.

Prof. H. said of this particular occasion: —

We may be quite sure that this Hall will be a center of deep interest to coming generations. Long after we shall have passed away will the men of New-York, as they survey these monuments, feel stimulated to engage in other noble enterprises by this work of their progenitors, and from many a distant part of the civilized world will men come here to solve their scientific questions, and to bring far-off regions into comparison with this. New-York, then, by her liberal patronage, has not only acquired an honorable name among those living in all civilized lands, but has secured the voice of History to transmit her fame to far-off generations.

SIR WILLIAM LOGAN ASKS "THE WAY TO ALBANY."

Sir William E. Logan, of Canada, in a brief speech acknowledged the services rendered by the New-York Survey to Canada. He should manifest ingratitude if he declined to unite in the joyful occasion of inaugurating the Museum which was to hold forever the evidence of the truth of its published results. The Survey of Canada had been ordered, and the Commission of five years twice renewed; and the last time, the provision for it was more than doubled. It happened to him, as Mr. Agassiz had said: after crossing the ocean first, the first thing he asked was, "Which is the way to Albany?" and when he arrived here, he found that with the aid of Prof. Hall's discoveries, he had only to take up the different formations as he had left them on the boundary line, and follow them into Canada. It was both a convenience and a necessity to adopt the New-York nomenclature, which was thus extended over an area six times as large as New-York. In Paris he heard De Vernier using the words Trenton and Niagara, as if they were household words. He was delighted to witness the impatience with which Barron inquired when the remaining volumes of the Paleontology of New-York would be published. Your Paleontological reputation, said he, has made New-York known, even among men not scientific, all over Europe. I hope you will not stop here, but will go on and give us in equally thorough, full, and magnificent style, the character of the Durassic and Cretaceous formations.

PROFESSOR HENRY ON DUTCHMEN.

Professor Henry was at a loss to know by what process they had arrived at the conclusion that seven men of science must be substituted to fill the place of one distinguished statesman whom they had expected to hear. He prided [8]himself on his Albany nativity. He was proud of the old Dutch character, that was the substratum of the city. The Dutch are hard to be moved, but when they do start their momentum is not as other men's in proportion to the velocity, but as the square of the velocity. So when the Dutchman goes three times as fast, he has nine times the force of another man. The Dutchman has an immense potentia agency, but it wants a small spark of Yankee enterprise to touch it off. In this strain the Professor continued, making his audience very merry, and giving them a fine chance to express themselves with repeated explosions of laughter.

PROFESSOR DAVIES ON THE PRACTICAL NATURE OF SCIENCE.

Prof. Charles Davies was introduced by Ex-Governor Seymour, and spoke briefly, but humorously and very much to the point, in defense of the practical character of scientific researches. He said that to one accustomed to speak only on the abstract quantities of number and space, this was an unusual occasion, and this an unusual audience; and inquired how he could discuss the abstract forms of geometry, when he saw before him, in such profusion, the most beautiful real forms that Providence has vouchsafed to the life of man. He proposed to introduce and develop but a single train of thought—the unchangeable connection between what in common language is called the theoretical and practical, but in more technical phraseology, the ideal and the actual. The actual, or true practical, consists in the uses of the forces of nature, according to the laws of nature; and here we must distinguish between it and the empirical, which uses, or attempts to use, those forces, without a knowledge of the laws. The true practical, therefore, is the result, or actual, of an antecedent ideal. The ideal, full and complete, must exist in the mind before the actual can be brought forth according to the laws of science. Who, then, are the truly practical men of our age? Are they not those who are engaged most laboriously and successfully in investigating the great laws? Are they not those who are pressing out the boundaries of knowledge, and conducting the mind into new and unexplored regions, where there may yet be discovered a California of undeveloped thought? Is not the gentleman from Massachusetts (Professor Agassiz) the most practical man in our country in the department of Natural History, not because he has collected the greatest number of specimens, but because he has laid open to us all the laws of the animal kingdom? Are the formulas written on the black-board by the gentleman from Cambridge (Prof. Pierce) of no practical value, because they cannot be read by the uninstructed eye? A single line may contain the elements of the motions of all the heavenly bodies; and the eye of science, taking its stand-point at the center of gravity of the system, will see in the equation the harmonious revolutions of all the bodies which circle the heavens. It is such labors and such generalizations that have rendered his name illustrious in the history of mathematical science. Is it of no practical value that the Chief of the Coast Survey (Prof. Bache), by a few characters written upon paper, at Washington, has determined the exact time of high and low tide in the harbor of Boston, and can determine, by a similar process, the exact times of high and low water at every point on the surface of the globe? Are not these results, the highest efforts of science, also of the greatest practical utility? And may we not, then, conclude that *there is nothing truly practical which is not the consequence of an antecedent ideal*?

Science is to art what the great fly-wheel and governor of a steam-engine are to the working part of the machinery—it guides, regulates, and controls the whole. Science and art are inseparably connected; like the Siamese Twins, they cannot be separated without producing the death of both.

How, then, are we to regard the superb specimens of natural history, which the liberality, the munificence; and the wisdom of our State have collected at the Capitol? They are the elements from which we can here determine all that belongs to the Natural History of our State; and may we not indulge the hope, [9]that science and genius will come here, and, striking them with a magic wand, cause the true practical to spring into immortal life?

Remarks were also uttered by Prof. Chester Dewey, President Anderson, and Rev. Dr. Cox.

And thus ended the Inauguration of the State Geological Hall.

We turn to the Observatory, in regular order of succession.

INAUGURATION OF DUDLEY OBSERVATORY.

The Inauguration of the Dudley Observatory took place under the same tent which was appropriated to the dedication of the Geological Hall, and on the day following that event. An immense audience was assembled, drawn by the announcement of Mr. Everett's Oration.

At a little past three o'clock the procession of *savans* arrived from the Assembly Chamber, escorted by the Burgesses Corps. Directly in front of the speaker's stand sat Mrs. Dudley, the venerable lady to whose munificence the world is indebted for this Observatory. She was dressed in an antique, olive-colored silk, with a figure of a lighter color, a heavy, red broché shawl, and her bonnet, cap, &c., after the strictest style of the old school. Her presence added a new point of interest.

Prayer having been uttered by Rev. Dr. Sprague, of Albany, Thomas W. Olcott, Esq., introduced to the audience Ex-Governor Washington Hunt, who spoke briefly in honor of the memory of Charles E. Dudley, whose widow has founded and in part endowed this Observatory with a liberality so remarkable.

Remarks were offered by Dr. B. A. Gould and Prof. A. D. Bache, and Judge Harris read the following letter from Mrs. Dudley, announcing another munificent donation in aid of the new Observatory— $50,000, in addition to the $25,000 which had been already expended in the construction of the building. The letter was received with shouts of applause, Prof. Agassiz rising and leading the vast assemblage in three vehement cheers in honor of Mrs. Dudley!

Albany, Thursday, Aug. 14, 1856.

To the Trustees of the Dudley Observatory:

Gentlemen,—I scarcely need refer in a letter to you to the modest beginning and gradual growth of the institution over which you preside, and of which you are the responsible guardians. But we have arrived at a period in its history when its inauguration gives to it and to you some degree of prominence, and which must stamp our past efforts with weakness and inconsideration, or exalt those of the future to the measure of liberality necessary to certain success.

You have a building erected and instruments engaged of unrivaled excellence; and it now remains to carry out the suggestion of the Astronomer Royal of England in giving permanency to the establishment. The very distinguished Professors Bache, Pierce, and Gould, state in a letter, which I have been permitted to see, that to expand this institution to the wants of American science and the honors of a national character, will require an investment which will yield annually not less than $10,000; and these gentlemen say, in the letter referred to, —

"If the greatness of your giving can rise to this occasion, as it has to all our previous suggestions, with such unflinching magnanimity, we promise you our earnest and hearty coöperation, and stake our reputation that the scientific success shall fill up the measure of your hopes and anticipations."

For the attainment of an object so rich in scientific reward and national glory, guaranteed by men with reputations as exalted and enduring as the skies upon which they are written, contributions should be general, and not confined to an individual or a place.

[10]

For myself, I offer, as my part of the required endowment, the sum of $50,000 in addition to the advances which I have already made; and, trusting that the name which you have given to the Observatory may not be regarded as an undeserved compliment, and that it will not diminish the public regard by giving to the institution a seemingly individual character,

I remain, Gentlemen, your obedient servant,
BLANDINA DUDLEY.

Judge Harris then introduced the Orator of the occasion, Hon. EdwardEverett, whose speech is given verbatim in these pages.

THE INSTRUMENTS OF THE DUDLEY OBSERVATORY.

During the Sessions of the American Association, the new Astronomical Instruments of Dudley Observatory were described in detail by Dr. B. A. Gould, who is the Astronomer in charge. We condense his statements: —

The Meridian Circle and Transit instrument were ordered from Pistor & Martins, the celebrated manufacturers of Berlin, by whom the new instrument at Ann Arbor was made. A number of improvements have been introduced in the Albany instruments, not perhaps all absolutely new, but an eclectic combination of late adaptations with new improvements. Dr. Gould made a distinction of modern astronomical instruments into two classes, the English and the German. The English is the massive type; the German, light and airy. The English instrument is the instrument of the engineer; the German, the instrument of the artist. In ordering the instruments for the Albany Observatory, the Doctor preferred the German type and discarded the heavier English. He instanced, as a specimen of the latter, the new instrument at Greenwich, recently erected under the superintendence of the Astronomer Royal. That instrument registers observations in single seconds; the Dudley instrument will register to tenths of seconds. That has six or eight microscopes; this has four. That has a gas lamp, by the light of which the graduations are read off; the Albany instrument has no lamp, and the Doctor considered the lamp a hazardous experiment, affecting the integrity of the experiment, not only by its radiant heat but by the currents of heated air which it produces. The diameter of the object-glass of the Albany instrument is 7½ French inches clear aperture, or 8 English inches, and the length of the tube 8 feet. He would have preferred an instrument in which the facilities of manipulation would have been greater, but was hampered by one proviso, upon which the Trustees of the institution insisted—that this should be the biggest instrument of its kind; and the instruction was obeyed. The glass was made by Chance, and ground by Pistor himself. The eye-piece is fitted with two micrometers, for vertical and horizontal observations. Another apparatus provides for the detection and measurement of the flexure of the tube. Much trouble was experienced in securing a good casting for the steel axis of the instrument. Three were found imperfect under the lathe, and the fourth was chosen; but even then the pivots were made in separate pieces, which were set in very deeply and welded. Dr. Gould said he had been requested by the gentlemen who had this enterprise in charge to suggest, as a mark of respect to a gentleman of Albany who was a munificent patron of Science, that this instrument be known as the Olcott Meridian Circle.

WHAT THE DUDLEY OBSERVATORY IS.

It stands a mile from the Capitol, in the city of Albany, upon the crest of a hill, so difficult of approach, as to be in reality a Hill of Science. There are two ways of getting to it. In both cases there are rail fences to be clambered over, and long grass to wade through, settlements to explore, and a clayey road to travel; but these are minor troubles. The elevation of the hill above tide-water [11]is, perhaps, 200 feet; its distance from the Capitol about a mile and a half. The view for miles is unimpeded; and the Observatory is belted about with woods and verdant lawns. There could not be a finer location or a purer air. The plateau contains some fifteen acres.

The Observatory is constructed in the form of a Latin cross. Its eastern arm is an apartment 22 by 24 feet, in which the meridian circle is to be placed. The western arm is a room of the same dimensions, intended for the transit instrument. From the north and south faces of both rooms are semi-circular apsides, projecting 6 feet 6 inches, containing the Collimator piers and the vertical openings for observation. The entire length of each room is, therefore, 37 feet. In the northern arm are placed the library, 23 feet by 27 feet; two computing rooms, 12 feet by 23 feet each; side entrance halls, staircases, &c. The southern arm contains the principal entrance, consisting of an arched colonnade of four Tuscan columns, surrounded by a pediment. A broad flight of stone steps leads to this colonnade; and through the entrance door beneath it to the main central hall, 28 feet square, in which are placed (in niches) the very beautiful electric clock and pendulum presented by Erastus Corning, Esq. The center of this hall is occupied by a massive pier of stone, 10 feet square, passing from the basement into the dome above, and intended for the support of the great heliometer. Directly opposite the entrance door is a large niche, in which it is proposed to place the bust of the late Mr. Dudley. Immediately above this hall is the equatorial room, a circular apartment, 22 feet 6 inches in diameter, and 24 feet high, covered by a low conical roof, in which and in the walls are the usual observing slits. The drum, or cylindrical portion, of this room is divided into two parts—the lower one fixed, the upper, revolving on cast-iron balls moving in grooved metal plates, can command the entire horizon.

The building is in two stories—the upper of brick, with freestone quoins, impost and window and door dressings, rests upon a rusticated basement of freestone, six feet high. The style adopted is the modern Italian, of which it is a very excellent specimen. The building has been completed some time; but, in consequence of the size of the instruments now procured being greater than that originally contemplated, sundry alterations were required in the Transit and Meridian Circle rooms. These consist of the semi-circular projections already mentioned, and which, by varying the outlines of the building, will add greatly to its beauty and picturesqueness.

The piers for the Meridian Circle and Transit have, after careful investigation, been procured from the Lockport quarries. The great density and uniformity of the structure of the stone, and the facility with which such large masses as are required for this purpose can be procured there, have induced the selection of these quarries. The stones will weigh from six and a half to eight tons each.

The main building was erected from the drawings of Messrs. Woollett and Ogden, Architects, Albany; the additions and the machinery have been designed by Mr. W. Hodgins, Civil Engineer; and the latter is now being constructed under his superintendence, in a very superior manner, at the iron works of Messrs. Pruyn and Lansing, Albany.

The entire building is a tasteful and elegant structure, much superior in architectural character to any other in America devoted to a similar purpose.

[12]

[13]

ORATION.

Fellow Citizens Of Albany:—

Assembled as we are, under your auspices, in this ancient and hospitable city, for an object indicative of a highly-advanced stage of scientific culture, it is natural, in the first place, to cast a historical glance at the past. It seems almost to surpass belief, though an unquestioned fact, that more than a century should have passed away, after Cabot had discovered the coast of North America for England, before any knowledge was gained of the noble river on which your city stands, and which was destined by Providence to determine, in after times, the position of the commercial metropolis of the Continent. It is true that Verazzano, a bold and sagacious Florentine navigator, in the service of France, had entered the Narrows in 1524, which he describes as a very large river, deep at its mouth, which forced its way through steep hills to the sea; but though he, like all the naval adventurers of that age, was sailing westward in search of a shorter passage to India, he left this part of the coast without any attempt to ascend the river; nor can it be gathered from his narrative that he believed it to penetrate far into the interior.

VOYAGE OF HENDRICK HUDSON.

Near a hundred years elapsed before that great thought acquired substance and form. In the spring of 1609, the heroic but unfortunate Hudson, one of the brightest names in the history of English maritime adventure, but then in the employment of the Dutch East India Company, in a vessel of eighty tons, bearing the very astronomical name of the *Half Moon*, having been stopped by the ice in the Polar Sea, in the attempt to reach the East by the way of Nova Zembla, struck over to the coast of America in a high northern latitude. He then stretched down southwardly to the entrance of Chesapeake Bay (of which he had gained a knowledge from the charts and descriptions of his friend, Captain Smith), thence returning to the north, entered Delaware Bay, standing out again to sea, arrived on the second of September in sight of the "high hills" of Neversink, pronouncing it "a good land to fall in with, and a pleasant land to see;" and, on the following morning, sending his boat before him to sound the way, passed Sandy Hook, [14]and there came to anchor on the third of September, 1609; two hundred and forty-seven years ago next Wednesday. What an event, my friends, in the history of American population, enterprise, commerce, intelligence, and power—the dropping of that anchor at Sandy Hook!

DISCOVERY OF THE HUDSON RIVER.

Here he lingered a week, in friendly intercourse with the natives of New Jersey, while a boat's company explored the waters up to Newark Bay. And now the great question. Shall he turn back, like Verazzano, or ascend the stream? Hudson was of a race not prone to turn back, by sea or by land. On the eleventh of September he raised the anchor of the *Half Moon*, passed through the Narrows, beholding on both sides "as beautiful a land as one can tread on;" and floated cautiously and slowly up the noble stream—the first ship that ever rested on its bosom. He passed the Palisades, nature's dark basaltic Malakoff, forced the iron gateway of the Highlands, anchored, on the fourteenth, near West Point; swept onward and upward, the following day, by grassy meadows and tangled slopes, hereafter to be covered with smiling villages;—by elevated banks and woody heights, the destined site of towns and cities—of Newburg, Poughkeepsie, Catskill;—on the evening of the fifteenth arrived opposite "the mountains which lie from the river side," where he found "a very loving people and very old men;" and the day following sailed by the spot hereafter to be honored by his own illustrious name. One more day wafts him up between Schodac and Castleton; and here he landed and passed a day with the natives,—greeted with all sorts of barbarous hospitality,—the land "the finest for cultivation he ever set foot on," the natives so kind and gentle, that when they found he would not remain with them over night, and feared that he left them—poor children of nature!—because he was afraid of their weapons,—he, whose quarter-deck was heavy with ordnance,—they "broke their arrows in pieces, and threw them in the fire." On the following morning, with the early flood-tide, on the 19th of September, 1609, the *Half Moon* "ran higher up, two leagues above the Shoals," and came to anchor in deep water, near the site of the present city of Albany. Happy if he could have closed his gallant career on the banks of the stream which so justly bears his name, and thus have escaped the sorrowful and mysterious catastrophe which awaited him the next year!

CHAMPLAIN'S VOYAGE AND THE GROWTH OF COLONIES.

But the discovery of your great river and of the site of your ancient city, is not the only event which renders the year 1609 memorable in the annals of America and the world. It was one of those years in which a sort of sympathetic movement toward great results unconsciously pervades the races and the minds of men. While Hudson discovered this mighty river [15]and this vast region for the Dutch East India Company, Champlain, in the same year, carried the lilies of France to the beautiful lake which bears his name on your northern limits; the languishing establishments of England in Virginia were strengthened by the second charter granted to that colony; the little church of Robinson removed from Amsterdam to Leyden, from which, in a few years, they went forth, to lay the foundations of New England on Plymouth Rock; the seven United Provinces of the Netherlands, after that terrific struggle of forty years (the commencement of which has just been embalmed in a record worthy of the great event by an American historian) wrested from Spain the virtual acknowledgment of their independence, in the Twelve Years' Truce; and James the First, in the same year, granted to the British East India Company their first permanent charter, — corner-stone of an empire destined in two centuries to overshadow the East.

GALILEO'S DISCOVERIES

One more incident is wanting to complete the list of the memorable occurrences which signalize the year 1609, and one most worthy to be remembered by us on this occasion. Cotemporaneously with the events which I have enumerated — eras of history, dates of empire, the starting-point in some of the greatest political, social, and moral revolutions in our annals, an Italian astronomer, who had heard of the magnifying glasses which had been made in Holland, by which distant objects could be brought seemingly near, caught at the idea, constructed a telescope, and pointed it to the heavens. Yes, my friends, in the same year in which Hudson discovered your river and the site of your ancient town, in which Robinson made his melancholy hegira from Amsterdam to Leyden, Galileo Galilei, with a telescope, the work of his own hands, discovered the phases of Venus and the satellites of Jupiter; and now, after the lapse of less than two centuries and a half, on a spot then embosomed in the wilderness — the covert of the least civilized of all the races of men — we are assembled — descendants of the Hollanders, descendants of the Pilgrims, in this ancient and prosperous city, to inaugurate the establishment of a first-class Astronomical Observatory.

EARLY DAYS OF ALBANY.

One more glance at your early history. Three years after the landing of the Pilgrims at Plymouth, Fort Orange was erected, in the center of what is now the business part of the city of Albany; and, a few years later, the little hamlet of Beverswyck began to nestle under its walls. Two centuries ago, my Albanian friends, this very year, and I believe this very month of August, your forefathers assembled, not to inaugurate an observatory, but to lay the foundations of a new church, in the place of the rude cabin which had hitherto served them in that capacity. It was built at the intersection [16]of Yonker's and Handelaar's, better known to you as State and Market streets. Public and private liberality coöperated in the important work. The authorities at the Fort gave fifteen hundred guilders; the patroon of that early day, with the liberality coëval with the name and the race, contributed a thousand; while the inhabitants, for whose benefit it was erected, whose numbers were small and their resources smaller, contributed twenty beavers "for the purchase of an oaken pulpit in Holland." Whether the largest part of this subscription was bestowed by some liberal benefactress, tradition has not informed us.

NEW AMSTERDAM

Nor is the year 1656 memorable in the annals of Albany alone. In that same year your imperial metropolis, then numbering about three hundred inhabitants, was first laid out as a city, by the name of New Amsterdam.[A] In eight years more, New Netherland becomes New York; Fort Orange and its dependent hamlet assumes the name of Albany. A century of various fortune succeeds; the scourge of French and Indian war is rarely absent from the land; every shock of European policy vibrates with electric rapidity across the Atlantic; but the year 1756 finds a population of 300,000 in your growing province. Albany, however, may still be regarded almost as a frontier settlement. Of the twelve counties into which the province was divided a hundred years ago, the county of Albany comprehended all that lay north and west of the city; and the city itself contained but about three hundred and fifty houses.

[A] These historical notices are, for the most part, abridged from Mr. Brodhead's excellent history of New York.

TWO HUNDRED YEARS.

One more century; another act in the great drama of empire; another French and Indian War beneath the banners of England; a successful Revolution, of which some of the most momentous events occurred within your limits; a union of States; a Constitution of Federal Government; your population carried to the St. Lawrence and the great Lakes, and their waters poured into the Hudson; your territory covered with a net-work of canals and railroads, filled with life and action, and power, with all the works of peaceful art and prosperous enterprise with all the institutions which constitute and advance the civilization of the age; its population exceeding that of the Union at the date of the Revolution; your own numbers twice as large as those of the largest city of that day, you have met together, my Friends, just two hundred years since the erection of the little church of Beverswyck, to dedicate a noble temple of science and to take a becoming public notice of the establishment of an institution, destined, as we trust, to exert a beneficial influence on the progress of useful knowledge at home and abroad, and through that on the general cause of civilization.

[17]

SCIENTIFIC PROGRESS.

You will observe that I am careful to say the progress of science "at home and abroad;" for the study of Astronomy in this country has long since, I am happy to add, passed that point where it is content to repeat the observations and verify the results of European research. It has boldly and successfully entered the field of original investigation, discovery, and speculation; and there is not now a single department of the science in which the names of American observers and mathematicians are not cited by our brethren across the water, side by side with the most eminent of their European contemporaries.

This state of things is certainly recent. During the colonial period and in the first generation after the Revolution, no department of science was, for obvious causes, very extensively cultivated in America—astronomy perhaps as much as the kindred branches. The improvement in the quadrant, commonly known as Hadley's, had already been made at Philadelphia by Godfrey, in the early part of the last century; and the beautiful invention of the collimating telescope was made at a later period by Rittenhouse, an astronomer of distinguished repute. The transits of Venus of 1761 and 1769 were observed, and orreries were constructed in different parts of the country; and some respectable scientific essays are contained and valuable observations are recorded in the early volumes of the Transactions of the Philosophical Society, at Philadelphia, and the American Academy of Arts and Sciences at Boston and Cambridge. But in the absence of a numerous class of men of science to encourage and aid each other, without observatories and without valuable instruments, little of importance could be expected in the higher walks of astronomical life.

AMERICAN OBSERVATIONS.

The greater the credit due for the achievement of an enterprise commenced in the early part of the present century, and which would reflect honor on the science of any country and any age; I mean the translation and commentary on Laplace's *Mécanique Celeste*, by Bowditch; a work of whose merit I am myself wholly unable to form an opinion, but which I suppose places the learned translator and commentator on a level with the ablest astronomers and geometers of the day. This work may be considered as opening a new era in the history of American science. The country was still almost wholly deficient in instrumental power; but the want was generally felt by men of science, and the public mind in various parts of the country began to be turned towards the means of supplying it. In 1825, President John Quincy Adams brought the subject of a National Observatory before Congress. Political considerations prevented its being favorably entertained at that time; and it was not till 1842, and as an incident of the exploring expedition, that an appropriation was made for a dépôt for the charts and [18]instruments of the Navy. On this modest basis has been reared the National Observatory at Washington; an institution which has already taken and fully sustains an honorable position among the scientific establishments of the age.

Besides the institution at Washington, fifteen or twenty observatories have within the last few years, been established in different parts of the country, some of them on a modest scale, for the gratification of the scientific taste and zeal of individuals, others on a broad foundation of expense and usefulness. In these establishments, public and private, the means are provided for the highest order of astronomical observation, research, and instruction. There is already in the country an amount of instrumental power (to which addition is constantly making), and of mathematical skill on the part of our men of science, adequate to a manly competition with their European contemporaries. The fruits are already before the world, in the triangulation of several of the States, in the great work of the Coast Survey, in the numerous scientific surveys of the interior of the Continent, in the astronomical department of the Exploring Expedition, in the scientific expedition to Chili, in the brilliant hydrographical labors of the Observatory at Washington, in the published observations of Washington and Cambridge, in the Journal conducted by the Nestor of American Science, now in its eighth lustrum; in the *Sidereal Messenger*, the *Astronomical Journal*, and the *National Ephemeris*; in the great chronometrical expeditions to determine the longitude of Cambridge, better ascertained than that of Paris was till within the last year; in the prompt rectification of the errors in the predicted elements of Neptune; in its identification with Lalande's missing star, and in the calculation of its ephemeris; in the discovery of the satellite of Neptune, of the eighth satellite of Saturn, and of the innermost of its rings; in the establishment, both by observation and theory, of the non-solid character of Saturn's rings; in the separation and measurement of many double and triple stars, amenable only to superior instrumental power, in the immense labor already performed in preparing star catalogues, and in numerous accurate observations of standard stars; in the diligent and successful observation of the meteoric showers; in an extensive series of magnetic observations; in the discovery of an asteroid and ten or twelve telescopic comets; in the resolution of nebulæ which had defied every thing in Europe but Lord Rosse's great reflector; in the application of electricity to the measurement of differences in longitude; in the ascertainment of the velocity of the electro-magnetic fluid, and its truly wonderful uses in recording astronomical observations. These are but a portion of the achievements of American astronomical science within fifteen or twenty years, and fully justify the most sanguine anticipations of its further progress.

How far our astronomers may be able to pursue their researches, will depend upon the resources of our public institutions, and the liberality of wealthy individuals in furnishing the requisite means. With the exception of the observatories at Washington and West Point, little can be done, or be [19]expected to be done, by the government of the Union or the States; but in this, as in every other department of liberal art and science, the great dependence,—and may I not add, the safe dependence?—as it ever has been, must continue to be upon the bounty of enlightened, liberal, and public-spirited individuals.

THE DUDLEY OBSERVATORY.

It is by a signal exercise of this bounty, my Friends, that we are called together to-day. The munificence of several citizens of this ancient city, among whom the first place is due to the generous lady whose name has with great propriety been given to the institution, has furnished the means for the foundation of the Dudley Observatory at Albany. On a commanding elevation on the northern edge of the city, liberally given for that purpose by the head of a family in which the patronage of science is hereditary, a building of ample dimensions has been erected, upon a plan which combines all the requisites of solidity, convenience, and taste. A large portion of the expense of the structure has been defrayed by Mrs. Blandina Dudley; to whose generosity, and that of several other public-spirited individuals, the institution is also indebted for the provision which has been made for an adequate supply of first-class instruments, to be executed by the most eminent makers in Europe and America; and which, it is confidently expected, will yield to none of their class in any observatory in the world.[A]

[A] Prof. Loomis, in *Harper's Magazine* for June, p. 49.

With a liberal supply of instrumental power; established in a community to whose intelligence and generosity its support may be safely confided, and whose educational institutions are rapidly realizing the conception of a university; countenanced by the gentleman who conducts the United States Coast Survey with such scientific skill and administrative energy; committed to the immediate supervision of an astronomer to whose distinguished talent had been added the advantage of a thorough scientific education in the most renowned universities of Europe, and who, as the editor of the *American Astronomical Journal*, has shown himself to be fully qualified for the high trust;—under these favorable circumstances, the Dudley Observatory at Albany takes its place among the scientific foundations of the country and the world.

WONDERS OF ASTRONOMY.

It is no affected modesty which leads me to express the regret that this interesting occasion could not have taken place under somewhat different auspices. I feel that the duty of addressing this great and enlightened assembly, comprising so much of the intelligence of the community and of the science of the country, ought to have been elsewhere assigned; that it should have devolved upon some one of the eminent persons, many of whom I see before me, to whom you have been listening the past week, who, as observers [20]and geometers, could have treated the subject with a master's power; astronomers, whose telescopes have penetrated the depths of the heavens, or mathematicians, whose analysis unthreads the maze of their wondrous mechanism. If, instead of commanding, as you easily could have done, qualifications of this kind, your choice has rather fallen on one making no pretensions to the honorable name of a man of science,—but whose delight it has always been to turn aside from the dusty paths of active life, for an interval of recreation in the green fields of sacred nature in all her kingdoms,—it is, I presume, because you have desired on an occasion of this kind, necessarily of a popular character, that those views of the subject should be presented which address themselves to the general intelligence of the community, and not to its select scientific circles. There is, perhaps, no branch of science which to the same extent as astronomy exhibits phenomena which, while they task the highest powers of philosophical research, are also well adapted to arrest the attention of minds barely tinctured with scientific culture, and even to teach the sensibilities of the wholly uninstructed observer. The profound investigations of the chemist into the ultimate constitution of material nature, the minute researches of the physiologist into the secrets of animal life, the transcendental logic of the geometer, clothed in a notation, the very sight of which terrifies the uninitiated, — are lost on the common understanding. But the unspeakable glories of the rising and the setting sun; the serene majesty of the moon, as she walks in full-orbed brightness through the heavens; the soft witchery of the morning and the evening star; the imperial splendors of the firmament on a bright, unclouded night; the comet, whose streaming banner floats over half the sky, — these are objects which charm and astonish alike the philosopher and the peasant, the mathematician who weighs the masses and defines the orbits of the heavenly bodies, and the untutored observer who sees nothing beyond the images painted upon the eye.

WHAT IS AN ASTRONOMICAL OBSERVATORY?

An astronomical observatory, in the general acceptation of the word, is a building erected for the reception and appropriate use of astronomical instruments, and the accommodation of the men of science employed in making and reducing observations of the heavenly bodies. These instruments are mainly of three classes, to which I believe all others of a strictly astronomical character may be referred.

1. The instruments by which the heavens are inspected, with a view to discover the existence of those celestial bodies which are not visible to the naked eye (beyond all comparison more numerous than those which are), and the magnitude, shapes, and other sensible qualities, both of those which are and those which are not thus visible to the unaided sight. The instruments of this class are designated by the general name of Telescope, and are of two kinds, — the refracting telescope, which derives its magnifying power [21]from a system of convex lenses; and the reflecting telescope, which receives the image of the heavenly body upon a concave mirror.

2d. The second class of instruments consists of those which are designed principally to measure the angular distances of the heavenly bodies from each other, and their time of passing the meridian. The transit instrument, the meridian circle, the mural circle, the heliometer, and the sextant, belong to this class. The brilliant discoveries of astronomy are, for the most part, made with the first class of instruments; its practical results wrought out by the second.

3d. The third class contains the clock, with its subsidiary apparatus, for measuring the time and making its subdivisions with the greatest possible accuracy; indispensable auxiliary of all the instruments, by which the positions and motions of the heavenly bodies are observed, and measured, and recorded.

THE TELESCOPE.

The telescope may be likened to a wondrous cyclopean eye, endued with superhuman power, by which the astronomer extends the reach of his vision to the further heavens, and surveys galaxies and universes compared with which the solar system is but an atom floating in the air. The transit may be compared to the measuring rod which he lays from planet to planet, and from star to star, to ascertain and mark off the heavenly spaces, and transfer them to his note-book; the clock is that marvelous apparatus by which he equalizes and divides into nicely measured parts a portion of that unconceived infinity of duration, without beginning and without end, in which all existence floats as on a shoreless and bottomless sea.

In the contrivance and the execution of these instruments, the utmost stretch of inventive skill and mechanical ingenuity has been put forth. To such perfection have they been carried, that a single second of magnitude or space is rendered a distinctly visible and appreciable quantity. "The arc of a circle," says Sir J. Herschell, "subtended by one second, is less than the 200,000th part of the radius, so that on a circle of six feet in diameter, it would occupy no greater linear extent than 1-5700 part of an inch, a quantity requiring a powerful microscope to be discerned at all."[A] The largest body in our system, the sun, whose real diameter is 882,000 miles, subtends, at a distance of 95,000,000 miles, but an angle of little more than 32; while so admirably are the best instruments constructed, that both in Europe and America a satellite of Neptune, an object of comparatively inconsiderable diameter, has been discovered at a distance of 2,850 millions of miles.

[A]*Outlines*, § 131.

UTILITY OF ASTRONOMICAL OBSERVATIONS.

The object of an observatory, erected and supplied with instruments of this admirable construction, and at proportionate expense, is, as I have [22]already intimated, to provide for an accurate and systematic survey of the heavenly bodies, with a view to a more correct and extensive acquaintance with those already known, and as instrumental power and skill in using it increase, to the discovery of bodies hitherto invisible, and in both classes to the determination of their distances, their relations to each other, and the laws which govern their movements.

Why should we wish to obtain this knowledge? What inducement is there to expend large sums of money in the erection of observatories, and in furnishing them with costly instruments, and in the support of the men of science employed in making, discussing, and recording, for successive generations, those minute observations of the heavenly bodies?

In an exclusively scientific treatment of this subject, an inquiry into its utilitarian relations would be superfluous—even wearisome. But on an occasion like the present, you will not, perhaps, think it out of place if I briefly answer the question, What is the use of an observatory, and what benefit may be expected from the operations of such an establishment in a community like ours?

1. In the first place, then, we derive from the observations of the heavenly bodies which are made at an observatory, our only adequate measures of time, and our only means of comparing the time of one place with the time of another. Our artificial time-keepers—clocks, watches, and chronometers—however ingeniously contrived and admirably fabricated, are but a transcript, so to say, of the celestial motions, and would be of no value without the means of regulating them by observation. It is impossible for them, under any circumstances, to escape the imperfection of all machinery the work of human hands; and the moment we remove with our time-keeper east or west, it fails us. It will keep home time alone, like the fond

traveler who leaves his heart behind him. The artificial instrument is of incalculable utility, but must itself be regulated by the eternal clock-work of the skies.

RELATIONS BETWEEN NATURAL PHENOMENA AND DAILY LIFE.

This single consideration is sufficient to show how completely the daily business of life is affected and controlled by the heavenly bodies. It is they—and not our main-springs, our expansion balances, and our compensation pendulums—which give us our time. To reverse the line of Pope:

"'Tis with our watches as our judgments;—none

Go just alike, but each believes his own."

But for all the kindreds and tribes and tongues of men—each upon their own meridian—from the Arctic pole to the equator, from the equator to the Antarctic pole, the eternal sun strikes twelve at noon, and the glorious constellations, far up in the everlasting belfries of the skies, chime twelve at midnight;—twelve for the pale student over his flickering lamp; twelve [23]amid the flaming glories of Orion's belt, if he crosses the meridian at that fated hour; twelve by the weary couch of languishing humanity; twelve in the star-paved courts of the Empyrean; twelve for the heaving tides of the ocean; twelve for the weary arm of labor; twelve for the toiling brain; twelve for the watching, waking, broken heart; twelve for the meteor which blazes for a moment and expires; twelve for the comet whose period is measured by centuries; twelve for every substantial, for every imaginary thing, which exists in the sense, the intellect, or the fancy, and which the speech or thought of man, at the given meridian, refers to the lapse of time.

Not only do we resort to the observation of the heavenly bodies for the means of regulating and rectifying our clocks, but the great divisions of day and month and year are derived from the same source. By the constitution of our nature, the elements of our existence are closely connected with celestial times. Partly by his physical organization, partly by the experience of the race from the dawn of creation, man as he is, and the times and seasons of the heavenly bodies, are part and parcel of one system. The first great division of time, the day-night (nychthemerum), for which we have no precise synonym in our language, with its primal alternation of waking and sleeping, of labor and rest, is a vital condition of the existence of such a creature as man. The revolution of the year, with its various incidents of summer and winter, and seed-time and harvest, is not less involved in our social, material, and moral progress. It is true that at the poles, and on the equator, the effects of these revolutions are variously modified or wholly disappear; but as the necessary consequence, human life is extinguished at the poles, and on the equator attains only a languid or feverish development. Those latitudes only in which the great motions and cardinal positions of the earth exert a mean influence, exhibit man in the harmonious expansion of his powers. The lunar period, which lies at the foundation of the *month*, is less vitally connected with human existence and development; but is proved by the experience of every age and race to be eminently conducive to the progress of civilization and culture.

But indispensable as are these heavenly measures of time to our life and progress, and obvious as are the phenomena on which they rest, yet owing to the circumstance that, in the economy of nature, the day, the month, and the year are not exactly commensurable, some of the most difficult questions in practical astronomy are those by which an accurate division of time, applicable to the various uses of life, is derived from the observation of the heavenly bodies. I have no doubt that, to the Supreme Intelligence which created and rules the universe, there is a harmony hidden to us in the numerical relation to each other of days, months, and years; but in our ignorance of that harmony, their practical adjustment to each other is a work of difficulty. The great embarrassment which attended the reformation of the calendar, after the error of the Julian period had, in the lapse of centuries, reached ten (or rather twelve) days, sufficiently illustrates this [24]remark. It is most true that scientific difficulties did not form the chief obstacle. Having been proposed under the auspices of the Roman pontiff, the Protestant world, for a century and more, rejected the new style. It was in various places the subject of controversy, collision, and bloodshed.[A] It was not adopted in England till nearly two centuries after its introduction at Rome; and in the country of Struve and the Pulkova equatorial, they persist at the present day in adding eleven minutes and twelve seconds to the length of the tropical year.

[A] Stern's "*Himmelskunde,*" p. 72.

GEOGRAPHICAL SCIENCE.

2. The second great practical use of an Astronomical Observatory is connected with the science of geography. The first page of the history of our Continent declares this truth. Profound meditation on the sphericity of the earth was one of the main reasons which led Columbus to undertake his momentous voyage; and his thorough acquaintance with the astronomical science of that day was, in his own judgment, what enabled him to overcome the almost innumerable obstacles which attended its prosecution.[A] In return, I find that Copernicus in the very commencement of his immortal work *De Revolutionibus Orbium Cœlestium*, fol. 2, appeals to the discovery of America as completing the demonstration of the sphericity of the earth. Much of our knowledge of the figure, size, density, and position of the earth, as a member of the solar system, is derived from this science; and it furnishes us the means of performing the most important operations of practical geography. Latitude and longitude, which lie at the basis of all descriptive geography, are determined by observation. No map deserves the name, on which the position of important points has not been astronomically determined. Some even of our most important political and administrative arrangements depend upon the coöperation of this science. Among these I may mention the land system of the United States, and the determination of the boundaries of the country. I believe that till it was done by the Federal Government, a uniform system of mathematical survey had never in any country been applied to an extensive territory. Large grants and sales of public land took place before the Revolution, and in the interval between the peace and the adoption of the Constitution; but the limits of these grants and sales were ascertained by sensible objects, by trees, streams, rocks, hills, and by reference to adjacent portions of territory, previously surveyed. The uncertainty of boundaries thus defined, was a never-failing source of litigation. Large tracts of land in the Western country, granted by Virginia under this old system of special and local survey, were covered with conflicting claims; and the controversies

to which they gave rise formed no small part of the business of the Federal Court after its organization. But the adoption of the present land-system brought order out of chaos. The entire public domain is now scientifically[25] surveyed before it is offered for sale; it is laid off into ranges, townships, sections, and smaller divisions, with unerring accuracy, resting on the foundation of base and meridian lines; and I have been informed that under this system, scarce a case of contested location and boundary has ever presented itself in court. The General Land Office contains maps and plans, in which every quarter-section of the public land is laid down with mathematical precision. The superficies of half a continent is thus transferred in miniature to the bureaus of Washington; while the local Land Offices contain transcripts of these plans, copies of which are furnished to the individual purchaser. When we consider the tide of population annually flowing into the public domain, and the immense importance of its efficient and economical administration, the utility of this application of Astronomy will be duly estimated.

[A] Humboldt, *Histotre de la Geographie*, &c., Tom. 1, page 71.

I will here venture to repeat an anecdote, which I heard lately from a son of the late Hon. Timothy Pickering. Mr. Octavius Pickering, on behalf of his father, had applied to Mr. David Putnam of Marietta, to act as his legal adviser, with respect to certain land claims in the Virginia Military district, in the State of Ohio. Mr. Putnam declined the agency. He had had much to do with business of that kind, and found it beset with endless litigation. "I have never," he added, "succeeded but in a single case, and that was a location and survey made by General Washington before the Revolution; and I am not acquainted with any surveys, except those made by him, but what have been litigated."

At this moment, a most important survey of the coast of the United States is in progress, an operation of the utmost consequence, in reference to the commerce, navigation, and hydrography of the country. The entire work, I need scarce say, is one of practical astronomy. The scientific establishment which we this day inaugurate is looked to for important coöperation in this great undertaking, and will no doubt contribute efficiently to its prosecution.

Astronomical observation furnishes by far the best means of defining the boundaries of States, especially when the lines are of great length and run through unsettled countries. Natural indications, like rivers and mountains, however indistinct in appearance, are in practice subject to unavoidable error. By the treaty of 1783, a boundary was established between the United States and Great Britain, depending chiefly on the course of rivers and highlands dividing the waters which flow into the Atlantic Ocean from those which flow into the St. Lawrence. It took twenty years to find out which river was the true St. Croix, that being the starting point. England then having made the extraordinary discovery that the Bay of Fundy is not a part of the Atlantic Ocean, forty years more were passed in the unsuccessful attempt to re-create the highlands which this strange theory had annihilated; and just as the two countries were on the verge of a war, the controversy was settled by compromise. Had the boundary been accurately [26]described by lines of latitude and longitude, no dispute could have arisen. No dispute arose as to the boundary between the United States and Spain, and her successor, Mexico, where it runs through untrodden deserts and over pathless mountains along the 42d degree of latitude. The identity of rivers may be disputed, as in the case of the St. Croix; the course of mountain chains is too broad for a dividing line; the division of streams, as experience has shown, is uncertain; but a degree of latitude is written on the heavenly sphere, and nothing but an observation is required to read the record.

QUESTIONS OF BOUNDARY.

But scientific elements, like sharp instruments, must be handled with scientific accuracy. A part of our boundary between the British Provinces ran upon the forty-fifth degree of latitude; and about forty years ago, an expensive fortress was commenced by the government of the United States, at Rouse's Point, on Lake Champlain, on a spot intended to be just within our limits. When a line came to be more carefully surveyed, the fortress turned out to be on the wrong side of the line; we had been building an expensive fortification for our neighbor. But in the general compromises of the Treaty of Washington by the Webster and Ashburton Treaty in 1842, the fortification was left within our limits.[A]

[A] Webster's Works. Vol. V., 110, 115.

Errors still more serious had nearly resulted, a few years since, in a war with Mexico. By the treaty of Guadalupe Hidalgo, in 1848, the boundary line between the United States and that country was in part described by reference to the town of El Paso, as laid down on a specified map of the United States, of which a copy was appended to the treaty. This boundary was to be surveyed and run by a joint commission of men of science. It soon appeared that errors of two or three degrees existed in the projection of the map. Its lines of latitude and longitude did not conform to the topography of the region; so that it became impossible to execute the text of the treaty. The famous Mesilla Valley was a part of the debatable ground; and the sum of $10,000,000, paid to the Mexican Government for that and for an additional strip of territory on the southwest, was the smart-money which expiated the inaccuracy of the map—the necessary result, perhaps, of the want of good materials for its construction.

It became my official duty in London, a few years ago, to apply to the British Government for an authentic statement of their claim to jurisdiction over New Zealand. The official *Gazette* for the 2d of October, 1840, was sent me from the Foreign Office, as affording the desired information. This number of the *Gazette* contained the proclamations issued by the Lieutenant Governor of New Zealand, "in pursuance of the instructions he received from the Marquis of Normanby, one of Her Majesty's principal Secretaries of [27]State," asserting the jurisdiction of his government over the islands of New Zealand, and declaring them to extend "from 34° 30' North to 47° 10' South latitude." It is scarcely necessary to say that south latitude was intended in both instances. This error of 69° of latitude, which would have extended the claim of British jurisdiction over the whole breadth of the Pacific, had, apparently, escaped the notice of that government.

COMMERCE AND NAVIGATION.

It would be easy to multiply illustrations in proof of the great practical importance of accurate scientific designations, drawn from astronomical observations, in various relations connected with boundaries, surveys, and other geographical purposes; but I must hasten to

3. A third important department, in which the services rendered by astronomy are equally conspicuous. I refer to commerce and navigation. It is mainly owing to the results of astronomical observation, that modern commerce has attained such a vast expansion, compared with that of the ancient world. I have already reminded you that accurate ideas in this respect contributed materially to the conception in the mind of Columbus of his immortal enterprise, and to the practical success with which it was conducted. It was mainly his skill in the use of astronomical instruments — imperfect as they were — which enabled him, in spite of the bewildering variation of the compass, to find his way across the ocean.

With the progress of the true system of the universe toward general adoption, the problem of finding the longitude at sea presented itself. This was the avowed object of the foundation of the observatory at Greenwich;[A] and no one subject has received more of the attention of astronomers, than those investigations of the lunar theory on which the requisite tables of the navigator are founded. The pathways of the ocean are marked out in the sky above. The eternal lights of the heavens are the only Pharos whose beams never fail, which no tempest can shake from its foundation. Within my recollection, it was deemed a necessary qualification for the master and the mate of a merchant-ship, and even for a prime hand, to be able to "work a lunar," as it was called. The improvements in the chronometer have in practice, to a great extent, superseded this laborious operation; but observation remains, and unquestionably will for ever remain, the only dependence for ascertaining the ship's time and deducting the longitude from the comparison of that time with the chronometer.

[A] Grant's *Physical Astronomy*, p. 460.

It may, perhaps, be thought that astronomical science is brought already to such a state of perfection that nothing more is to be desired, or at least that nothing more is attainable, in reference to such practicable applications as I have described. This, however, is an idea which generous minds will reject, in this, as in every other department of human knowledge. In astronomy, as in every thing else, the discoveries already made, theoretical or [28]practical, instead of exhausting the science, or putting a limit to its advancement, do but furnish the means and instruments of further progress. I have no doubt we live on the verge of discoveries and inventions, in every department, as brilliant as any that have ever been made; that there are new truths, new facts, ready to start into recognition on every side; and it seems to me there never was an age, since the dawn of time, when men ought to be less disposed to rest satisfied with the progress already made, than the age in which we live; for there never was an age more distinguished for ingenious research, for novel result, and bold generalization.

That no further improvement is desirable in the means and methods of ascertaining the ship's place at sea, no one I think will from experience be disposed to assert. The last time I crossed the Atlantic, I walked the quarter-deck with the officer in charge of the noble vessel, on one occasion, when we were driving along before a leading breeze and under a head of steam, beneath a starless sky at midnight, at the rate certainly of ten or eleven miles an hour. There is something sublime, but approaching the terrible, in such a scene;—the rayless gloom, the midnight chill,—the awful swell of the deep,—the dismal moan of the wind through the rigging, the all but volcanic fires within the hold of the ship. I scarce know an occasion in ordinary life in which a reflecting mind feels more keenly its hopeless dependence on irrational forces beyond its own control. I asked my companion how nearly he could determine his ship's place at sea under favorable circumstances. Theoretically, he answered, I think, within a mile;—practically and usually within three or four. My next question was, how near do you think we may be to Cape Race;—that dangerous headland which pushes its iron-bound unlighted bastions from the shore of Newfoundland far into the Atlantic,—first landfall to the homeward-bound American vessel. We must, said he, by our last observations and reckoning, be within three or four miles of Cape Race. A comparison of these two remarks, under the circumstances in which we were placed at the moment, brought my mind to the conclusion, that it is greatly to be wished that the means should be discovered of finding the ship's place more accurately, or that navigators would give Cape Race a little wider berth. But I do not remember that one of the steam packets between England and America was ever lost on that formidable point.

It appears to me by no means unlikely that, with the improvement of instrumental power, and of the means of ascertaining the ship's time with exactness, as great an advance beyond the present state of art and science in finding a ship's place at sea may take place, as was effected by the invention of the reflecting quadrant, the calculation of lunar tables, and the improved construction of chronometers.

BABBAGE'S DIFFERENCE MACHINE.

In the wonderful versatility of the human mind, the improvement, when made, will very probably be made by paths where it is least expected. The [29]great inducement to Mr. Babbage to attempt the construction of an engine by which astronomical tables could be calculated, and even printed, by mechanical means and with entire accuracy, was the errors in the requisite tables. Nineteen such errors, in point of fact, were discovered in an edition of Taylor's Logarithms printed in 1796; some of which might have led to the most dangerous results in calculating a ship's place. These nineteen errors, (of which one only was an error of the press), were pointed out in the *Nautical Almanac* for 1832. In one of these *errata* the seat of the error was stated to be in cosine of 14° 18' 3". Subsequent examination showed that there was an error of one second in this correction; and, accordingly, in the *Nautical Almanac* of the next year a new correction was necessary. But in making the new correction of one second, a new error was committed of ten degrees. Instead of cosine 14° 18' 2" the correction was printed cosine 4° 18' 2" making it still necessary, in some future edition of the *Nautical Almanac*, to insert an *erratum* in an *erratum* of the *errata* in Taylor's logarithms.[A]

[A] Edinburgh Review, Vol. LIX., 282.

In the hope of obviating the possibility of such errors, Mr. Babbage projected his calculating, or, as he prefers to call it, his difference machine. Although this extraordinary undertaking has been arrested, in consequence of the enormous expense attending its execution, enough has been achieved to show the mechanical possibility of constructing an engine of this kind, and even one of far higher powers, of which Mr. Babbage has matured the conception, devised the notation, and executed the drawings — themselves an imperishable monument of the genius of the author.

I happened on one occasion to be in company with this highly distinguished man of science, whose social qualities are as pleasing as his constructive talent is marvelous, when another eminent *savant*, Count Strzelecki, just returned from his Oriental and Australian tour, observed that he found among the Chinese, a great desire to know something more of Mr. Babbage's calculating machine, and especially whether, like their own *swampan*, it could be made to go into the pocket. Mr. Babbage good-humouredly observed that, thus far, he had been very much out of pocket with it.

INCREASED COMMAND OF INSTRUMENTAL POWER.

Whatever advances may be made in astronomical science, theoretical or applied, I am strongly inclined to think that they will be made in connection with an increased command of instrumental power. The natural order in which the human mind proceeds in the acquisition of astronomical knowledge is minute and accurate observation of the phenomena of the heavens, the skillful discussion and analysis of these observations, and sound philosophy in generalizing the results.

[30]

In pursuing this course, however, a difficulty presented itself, which for ages proved insuperable — and which to the same extent has existed in no other science, viz.: that all the leading phenomena are in their appearance delusive. It is indeed true that in all sciences superficial observation can only lead, except by chance, to superficial knowledge; but I know of no branch in which, to the same degree as in astronomy, the great leading phenomena are the reverse of true; while they yet appeal so strongly to the senses, that men who could foretell eclipses, and who discovered the precession of the equinoxes, still believed that the earth was at rest in the center of the universe, and that all the host of heaven performed a daily revolution about it as a center.

It usually happens in scientific progress, that when a great fact is at length discovered, it approves itself at once to all competent judges. It furnishes a solution to so many problems, and harmonizes with so many other facts,—that all the other *data* as it were crystallize at once about it. In modern times, we have often witnessed such an impatience, so to say, of great truths, to be discovered, that it has frequently happened that they have been found out simultaneously by more than one individual; and a disputed question of priority is an event of very common occurrence. Not so with the true theory of the heavens. So complete is the deception practiced on the senses, that it failed more than once to yield to the suggestion of the truth; and it was only when the visual organs were armed with an almost preternatural instrumental power, that the great fact found admission to the human mind.

THE COPERNICAN SYSTEM.

It is supposed that in the very dawn of science, Pythagoras or his disciples explained the apparent motion of the heavenly bodies about the earth by the diurnal revolution of the earth on its axis. But this theory, though bearing so deeply impressed upon it the great seal of truth, *simplicity*, was in such glaring contrast with the evidence of the senses, that it failed of acceptance in antiquity or the middle ages. It found no favor with minds like those of Aristotle, Archimedes, Hipparchus, Ptolemy, or any of the acute and learned Arabian or mediæval astronomers. All their ingenuity and all their mathematical skill were exhausted in the development of a wonderfully complicated and ingenious, but erroneous history. The great master truth, rejected for its simplicity, lay disregarded at their feet.

At the second dawn of science, the great fact again beamed into the mind of Copernicus. Now, at least, in that glorious age which witnessed the invention of printing, the great mechanical engine of intellectual progress, and the discovery of America, we may expect that this long-hidden revelation, a second time proclaimed, will command the assent of mankind. But the sensible phenomena were still too strong for the theory; the glorious delusion of the rising and the setting sun could not be overcome. Tycho de Brahe furnished his Observatory with instruments superior in number and quality to [31]all that had been collected before; but the great instrument of discovery, which, by augmenting the optic power of the eye, enables it to penetrate beyond the apparent phenomena, and to discern the true constitution of the heavenly bodies, was wanting at

Uranienburg. The observations of Tycho as discussed by Kepler, conducted that most fervid, powerful, and sagacious mind to the discovery of some of the most important laws of the celestial motions; but it was not till Galileo, at Florence, had pointed his telescope to the sky, that the Copernican system could be said to be firmly established in the scientific world.

THE HOME OF GALILEO.

On this great name, my Friends, assembled as we are to dedicate a temple to instrumental Astronomy, we may well pause for a moment.

There is much, in every way, in the city of Florence to excite the curiosity, to kindle the imagination, and to gratify the taste. Sheltered on the north by the vine-clad hills of Fiesoli, whose cyclopean walls carry back the antiquary to ages before the Roman, before the Etruscan power, the flowery city (Fiorenza) covers the sunny banks of the Arno with its stately palaces. Dark and frowning piles of mediæval structure; a majestic dome, the prototype of St. Peter's; basilicas which enshrine the ashes of some of the mightiest of the dead; the stone where Dante stood to gaze on the Campanile; the house of Michael Angelo, still occupied by a descendant of his lineage and name, his hammer, his chisel, his dividers, his manuscript poems, all as if he had left them but yesterday; airy bridges, which seem not so much to rest on the earth as to hover over the waters they span; the loveliest creations of ancient art, rescued from the grave of ages again to enchant the world; the breathing marbles of Michael Angelo, the glowing canvas of Raphael and Titian, museums filled with medals and coins of every age from Cyrus the younger, and gems and amulets and vases from the sepulchers of Egyptian Pharaohs coëval with Joseph, and Etruscan Lucumons that swayed Italy before the Romans,—libraries stored with the choicest texts of ancient literature,—gardens of rose and orange, and pomegranate, and myrtle,—the very air you breathe languid with music and perfume;—such is Florence. But among all its fascinations, addressed to the sense, the memory, and the heart, there was none to which I more frequently gave a meditative hour during a year's residence, than to the spot where Galileo Galilei sleeps beneath the marble door of Santa Croce; no building on which I gazed with greater reverence, than I did upon the modest mansion at Arcetri, villa at once and prison, in which that venerable sage, by command of the Inquisition, passed the sad closing years of his life. The beloved daughter on whom he had depended to smooth his passage to the grave, laid there before him; the eyes with which he had discovered worlds before unknown, quenched in blindness:

Ahime! quegli occhi si son fatti oscuri,

Che vider più di tutti i tempi antichi,

E luce fur dei secoli futuri.

[32]

That was the house, "where," says Milton (another of those of whom the world was not worthy), "I found and visited the famous Galileo, grown old — a prisoner to the Inquisition, for thinking on astronomy otherwise than as the Dominican and Franciscan licensers thought."[A] Great Heavens! what a tribunal, what a culprit, what a crime! Let us thank God, my Friends, that we live in the nineteenth century. Of all the wonders of ancient and modern art, statues and paintings, and jewels and manuscripts, — the admiration and the delight of ages, — there was nothing which I beheld with more affectionate awe than that poor, rough tube, a few feet in length, — the work of his own hands, — that very "optic glass," through which the "Tuscan Artist" viewed the moon,

"At evening, from the top of Fesolé,

Or in Valdarno, to descry new lands,

Rivers, or mountains, in her spotty globe."

that poor little spy-glass (for it is scarcely more) through which the human eye first distinctly beheld the surface of the moon — first discovered the phases of Venus, the satellites of Jupiter, and the seeming handles of Saturn — first penetrated the dusky depths of the heavens — first pierced the clouds of visual error, which, from the creation of the world, involved the system of the Universe.

[A] Prose Works, vol. 1, p. 213.

There are occasions in life in which a great mind lives years of rapt enjoyment in a moment. I can fancy the emotions of Galileo, when, first raising the newly-constructed telescope to the heavens, he saw fulfilled the grand prophecy of Copernicus, and beheld the planet Venus crescent like the moon. It was such another moment as that when the immortal printers of Mentz and Strasburg received the first copy of the Bible into their hands, the work of their divine art; like that when Columbus, through the gray dawn of the 12th of October, 1492 (Copernicus, at the age of eighteen, was then a student at Cracow), beheld the shores of San Salvador; like that when the law of gravitation first revealed itself to the intellect of Newton; like that when Franklin saw by the stiffening fibers of the hempen cord of his kite, that he held the lightning in his grasp; like that when Leverrier received back from Berlin the tidings that the predicted planet was found.

Yes, noble Galileo, thou art right, *E pur si muove.* "It does move." Bigots may make thee recant it; but it moves, nevertheless. Yes, the earth moves, and the planets move, and the mighty waters move, and the great sweeping tides of air move, and the empires of men move, and the world of thought moves, ever onward and upward to higher facts and bolder theories. The Inquisition may seal thy lips, but they can no more stop the progress of the great truth propounded by Copernicus, and demonstrated by thee, than they can stop the revolving earth.

Close now, venerable sage, that sightless, tearful eye; it has seen what man never before saw — it has seen enough. Hang up that poor little spy-glass — it has done its work. Not Herschell nor Rosse have, comparatively, [33]done more. Franciscans and Dominicans deride thy discoveries now; but the time will come when, from two hundred observatories in Europe and America, the glorious artillery of science shall nightly assault the skies, but they shall gain no conquests in those glittering fields before which thine shall be forgotten. Rest in peace, great Columbus of the heavens — like him scorned, persecuted, broken-hearted! — in other ages, in distant hemispheres, when the votaries of science, with solemn acts of consecration, shall dedicate their stately edifices to the cause of knowledge and truth, thy name shall be mentioned with honor.

NEW PERIODS IN ASTRONOMICAL SCIENCE.

It is not my intention, in dwelling with such emphasis upon the invention of the telescope, to ascribe undue importance, in promoting the advancement of science, to the increase of instrumental power. Too much, indeed, cannot be said of the service rendered by its first application in confirming and bringing into general repute the Copernican system; but for a considerable time, little more was effected by the wondrous instrument than the gratification of curiosity and taste, by the inspection of the planetary phases, and the addition of the rings and satellites of Saturn to the solar family. Newton, prematurely despairing of any further improvement in the refracting telescope, applied the principle of reflection; and the nicer observations now made, no doubt, hastened the maturity of his great discovery of the law of gravitation; but that discovery was the work of his transcendent genius and consummate skill.

With Bradley, in 1741, a new period commenced in instrumental astronomy, not so much of discovery as of measurement. The superior accuracy and minuteness with which the motions and distances of the heavenly bodies were now observed, resulted in the accumulation of a mass of new materials, both for tabular comparison and theoretical speculation. These materials formed the enlarged basis of astronomical science between Newton and Sir William Herschell. His gigantic reflectors introduced the astronomer to regions of space before unvisited — extended beyond all previous conception the range of the observed phenomena, and with it proportionably enlarged the range of constructive theory. The discovery of a new primary planet and its attendant satellites was but the first step of his progress into the labyrinth of the heavens. Cotemporaneously with his observations, the French astronomers, and especially La Place, with a geometrical skill scarcely, if at all, inferior to that of its great author, resumed the whole system of Newton, and brought every phenomenon observed since his time within his laws. Difficulties of fact, with which he struggled in vain, gave way to more accurate observations; and problems that defied the power of his analysis, yielded to the modern improvements of the calculus.

[34]

HERSCHELL'S NEBULAR THEORY.

But there is no *Ultima Thule* in the progress of science. With the recent augmentations of telescopic power, the details of the nebular theory, proposed by Sir W. Herschell with such courage and ingenuity, have been drawn in question. Many — most — of those milky patches in which he beheld what he regarded as cosmical matter, as yet in an unformed state, — the rudimental material of worlds not yet condensed, — have been resolved into stars, as bright and distinct as any in the firmament. I well recall the glow of satisfaction with which, on the 22d of September, 1847, being then connected with the University at Cambridge, I received a letter from the venerable director of the Observatory there, beginning with these memorable words: — "You will rejoice with me that the great nebula in Orion has yielded to the powers of our incomparable telescope! * * * It should be borne in mind that this nebula, and that of Andromeda [which has been also resolved at Cambridge], are the last strongholds of the nebular theory."[A]

[A]*Annals of the Observatory of Harvard College*, p. 121.

But if some of the adventurous speculations built by Sir William Herschell on the bewildering revelations of his telescope have been since questioned, the vast progress which has been made in sidereal astronomy, to which, as I understand, the Dudley Observatory will be particularly devoted, the discovery of the parallax of the fixed stars, the investigation of the interior relations of binary and triple systems of stars, the theories for the explanation of the extraordinary, not to say fantastic, shapes discerned in some of the nebulous systems — whirls and spirals radiating through spaces as vast as the orbit of Neptune;[A] the glimpses at systems beyond that to which our sun belongs; — these are all splendid results, which may fairly be attributed to the school of Herschell, and will for ever insure no secondary place to that name in the annals of science.

[A] See the remarkable memoir of Professor Alexander, "On the origin of the forms and the present condition of some of the clusters of stars, and several of the nebulæ," (Gould's *Astronomical Journal*, Vol. iii, p. 95.)

RELATIONSHIP OF THE LIBERAL ARTS.

In the remarks which I have hitherto made, I have had mainly in view the direct connection of astronomical science with the uses of life and the service of man. But a generous philosophy contemplates the subject in higher relations. It is a remark as old, at least, as Plato, and is repeated from him more than once by Cicero, that all the liberal arts have a common bond and relationship.[A] The different sciences contemplate as their immediate object the different departments of animate and inanimate nature; but this great system itself is but one, and its parts are so interwoven with each other, that the most extraordinary relations and unexpected analogies are [35]constantly presenting themselves; and arts and sciences seemingly the least connected, render to each other the most effective assistance.

[A] Archias, i.; De Oratore, iii., 21.

The history of electricity, galvanism, and magnetism, furnishes the most striking illustration of this remark. Commencing with the meteorological phenomena of our own atmosphere, and terminating with the observation of the remotest heavens, it may well be adduced, on an occasion like the present. Franklin demonstrated the identity of lightning and the electric fluid. This discovery gave a great impulse to electrical research, with little else in view but the means of protection from the thunder-cloud. A purely accidental circumstance led the physician Galvani, at Bologna, to trace the mysterious element, under conditions entirely novel, both of development and application. In this new form it became, in the hands of Davy, the instrument of the most extraordinary chemical operations; and earths and alkalis, touched by the creative wire, started up into metals that float on water, and kindle in the air. At a later period, the closest affinities are observed between electricity and magnetism, on the one hand; while, on the other, the relations of polarity are detected between acids and alkalis. Plating and gilding henceforth become electrical processes. In the last applications of the same subtle medium, it has become the messenger of intelligence across the land and beneath the sea; and is now employed by the astronomer to ascertain the difference of longitudes, to transfer the beats of the clock from one station to another, and to record the moment of his observations with automatic accuracy. How large a share has been borne by America in these magnificent discoveries and applications, among the most brilliant achievements of modern science, will sufficiently appear from the repetition of the names of Franklin, Henry, Morse, Walker, Mitchell, Lock, and Bond.

VERSATILITY OF GENIUS.

It has sometimes happened, whether from the harmonious relations to each other of every department of science, or from rare felicity of individual genius, that the most extraordinary intellectual versatility has been manifested by the same person. Although Newton's transcendent talent did not blaze out in childhood, yet as a boy he discovered great aptitude for mechanical contrivance. His water-clock, self-moving vehicle, and mill, were the wonder of the village; the latter propelled by a living mouse. Sir David Brewster represents the accounts as differing, whether the mouse was made to advance "by a string attached to its tail," or by "its unavailing attempts to reach a portion of corn placed above the wheel." It seems more reasonable to conclude that the youthful discoverer of the law of gravitation intended by the combination of these opposite attractions to produce a balanced movement. It is consoling to the average mediocrity of the race to perceive in these sportive assays, that the mind of Newton passed through the stage of boyhood. But emerging from boyhood, what a bound it made, as from earth to heaven! [36]Hardly commencing bachelor of arts, at the age of twenty-four, he untwisted the golden and silver threads of the solar spectrum, simultaneously or soon after conceived the method of fluxions, and arrived at the elemental idea of universal gravity before he had passed to his master's degree. Master of Arts indeed! That degree, if no other, was well bestowed. Universities are unjustly accused of fixing science in stereotype. That diploma is enough of itself to redeem the honors of academical parchment from centuries of learned dullness and scholastic dogmatism.

But the great object of all knowledge is to enlarge and purify the soul, to fill the mind with noble contemplations, to furnish a refined pleasure, and to lead our feeble reason from the works of nature up to its great Author and Sustainer. Considering this as the ultimate end of science, no branch of it can surely claim precedence of Astronomy. No other science furnishes such a palpable embodiment of the abstractions which lie at the foundation of our intellectual system; the great ideas of time, and space, and extension, and magnitude, and number, and motion, and power. How grand the conception of the ages on ages required for several of the secular equations of the solar system; of distances from which the light of a fixed star would not reach us in twenty millions of years, of magnitudes compared with which the earth is but a foot-ball; of starry hosts—suns like our own—numberless as the sands on the shore; of worlds and systems shooting through the infinite spaces, with a velocity compared with which the cannon-ball is a way-worn, heavy-paced traveler![A]

[A] Nichol's *Architecture of the Heavens*, p. 160.

THE SPECTACLE OF THE HEAVENS.

Much, however, as we are indebted to our observatories for elevating our conceptions of the heavenly bodies, they present, even to the unaided sight, scenes of glory which words are too feeble to describe. I had occasion, a few weeks since, to take the early train from Providence to Boston; and for this purpose rose at 2 o'clock in the morning. Every thing around was wrapped in darkness and hushed in silence, broken only by what seemed at that hour the unearthly clank and rush of the train. It was a mild, serene midsummer's night; the sky was without a cloud—the winds were whist. The moon, then in the last quarter, had just risen, and the stars shone with a spectral luster but little affected by her presence; Jupiter, two hours high, was the herald of the day; the Pleiades, just above the horizon, shed their sweet influence in the east; Lyra sparkled near the zenith; Andromeda veiled her newly discovered glories from the naked eye in the south; the steady Pointers, far beneath the pole, looked meekly up from the depths of the north to their sovereign.

Such was the glorious spectacle as I entered the train. As we proceeded, the timid approach of twilight became more perceptible; the intense blue of the sky began to soften, the smaller stars, like little children, went first to rest; the sister-beams of the Pleiades soon melted together; but the bright [37]constellations of the west and north remained unchanged. Steadily the wondrous transfiguration went on. Hands of angels hidden from mortal eyes shifted the scenery of the heavens; the glories of night dissolved into the glories of the dawn. The blue sky now turned more softly gray; the great watch-stars shut up their holy eyes; the east began to kindle. Faint streaks of purple soon blushed along the sky; the whole celestial concave was filled with the inflowing tides of the morning light, which came pouring down from above in one great ocean of radiance; till at length, as we reached the Blue Hills, a flash of purple fire blazed out from above the horizon, and turned the dewy tear-drops of flower and leaf into rubies and diamonds. In a few seconds the everlasting gates of the morning were thrown wide open, and the lord of day, arrayed in glories too severe for the gaze of man, began his course.

I do not wonder at the superstition of the ancient Magians, who in the morning of the world went up to the hill-tops of Central Asia, and ignorant of the true God, adored the most glorious work of his hand. But I am filled with amazement, when I am told that in this enlightened age, and in the heart of the Christian world, there are persons who can witness this daily manifestation of the power and wisdom of the Creator, and yet say in their hearts, "There is no God."

UNDISCOVERED BODIES.

Numerous as are the heavenly bodies visible to the naked eye, and glorious as are their manifestations, it is probable that in our own system there are great numbers as yet undiscovered. Just two hundred years ago this year, Huyghens announced the discovery of one satellite of Saturn, and expressed the opinion that the six planets and six satellites then known, and making up the perfect number of *twelve*, composed the whole of our planetary system. In 1729 an astronomical writer expressed the opinion that there might be other bodies in our system, but that the limit of telescopic power had been reached, and no further discoveries were likely to be made.[A] The orbit of one comet only had been definitively calculated. Since that time the power of the telescope has been indefinitely increased; two primary planets of the first class, ten satellites, and forty-three small planets revolving between Mars and Jupiter, have been discovered, the orbits of six or seven hundred comets, some of brief period, have been ascertained;—and it has been computed, that hundreds of thousands of these mysterious bodies wander through our system. There is no reason to think that all the primary planets, which revolve about the sun, have been discovered. An indefinite increase in the number of asteroids may be anticipated; while outside of Neptune, between our sun and the nearest fixed star, supposing the attraction of the sun to prevail through half the distance, there is room for ten more primary planets succeeding each other at distances increasing in a geometrical ratio. The first of these will, unquestionably, be discovered as soon as the perturbations of Neptune shall have been accurately observed; and with maps [38]of the heavens, on which the smallest telescopic stars are laid down, it may be discovered much sooner.

[A]*Memoirs of A.A.S.*, vol. iii, 275.

THE VASTNESS OF CREATION.

But it is when we turn our observation and our thoughts from our own system, to the systems which lie beyond it in the heavenly spaces, that we approach a more adequate conception of the vastness of creation. All analogy teaches us that the sun which gives light to us is but one of those countless stellar fires which deck the firmament, and that every glittering star in that shining host is the center of a system as vast and as full of subordinate luminaries as our own. Of these suns—centers of planetary systems—thousands are visible to the naked eye, millions are discovered by the telescope. Sir John Herschell, in the account of his operations at the Cape of Good Hope (p. 381) calculates that about five and a half millions of stars are visible enough to be *distinctly counted* in a twenty-foot reflector, in both hemispheres. He adds, that "the actual number is much greater, there can be little doubt." His illustrious father, estimated on one occasion that 125,000 stars passed through the field of his forty foot reflector in a quarter of an hour. This would give 12,000,000 for the entire circuit of the heavens, in a single telescopic zone; and this estimate was made under the assumption that the nebulæ were masses of luminous matter not yet condensed into suns.

These stupendous calculations, however, form but the first column of the inventory of the universe. Faint white specks are visible, even to the naked eye of a practiced observer in different parts of the heavens. Under high magnifying powers, several thousands of such spots are visible,—no longer however, faint, white specks, but

many of them resolved by powerful telescopes into vast aggrega-
tions of stars, each of which may, with propriety, be compared with
the milky way. Many of these nebulæ, however, resisted the power
of Sir Wm. Herschell's great reflector, and were, accordingly, still
regarded by him as masses of unformed matter, not yet condensed
into suns. This, till a few years since, was, perhaps, the prevailing
opinion; and the nebular theory filled a large space in modern astronomical science. But with the increase of instrumental power,
especially under the mighty grasp of Lord Rosse's gigantic reflector,
and the great refractors at Pulkova and Cambridge, the most irre-
solvable of these nebulæ have given way; and the better opinion
now is, that every one of them is a galaxy, like our own milky way,
composed of millions of suns. In other words, we are brought to the
bewildering conclusion that thousands of these misty specks, the
greater part of them too faint to be seen with the naked eye, are, not
each a universe like our solar system, but each a "swarm" of universes of unappreciable magnitude.[A] The mind sinks, overpow-
ered by the contemplation. We repeat the words, but they no longer
convey distinct ideas to the understanding.

[A] Humboldt's *Cosmos*, iii. 41.

[39]

CONCEPTIONS OF THE UNIVERSE.

But these conclusions, however vast their comprehension, carry
us but another step forward in the realms of sidereal astronomy. A
proper motion in space of our sun, and of the fixed stars as we call
them, has long been believed to exist. Their vast distances only pre-
vent its being more apparent. The great improvement of instruments of measurement within the last generation has not only established the existence of this motion, but has pointed to the region in
the starry vault around which our whole solar and stellar system,
with its myriad of attendant planetary worlds, appears to be performing a mighty revolution. If, then, we assume that outside of the
system to which we belong and in which our sun is but a star like
Aldebaran or Sirius, the different nebulæ of which we have spo-
ken,—thousands of which spot the heavens—constitute a distinct
family of universes, we must, following the guide of analogy, at-
tribute to each of them also, beyond all the revolutions of their indi-

vidual attendant planetary systems, a great revolution, comprehending the whole; while the same course of analogical reasoning would lead us still further onward, and in the last analysis, require us to assume a transcendental connection between all these mighty systems—a universe of universes, circling round in the infinity of space, and preserving its equilibrium by the same laws of mutual attraction which bind the lower worlds together.

It may be thought that conceptions like these are calculated rather to depress than to elevate us in the scale of being; that, banished as he is by these contemplations to a corner of creation, and there reduced to an atom, man sinks to nothingness in this infinity of worlds. But a second thought corrects the impression. These vast contemplations are well calculated to inspire awe, but not abasement. Mind and matter are incommensurable. An immortal soul, even while clothed in "this muddy vesture of decay," is in the eye of God and reason, a purer essence than the brightest sun that lights the depths of heaven. The organized human eye, instinct with life and soul, which, gazing through the telescope, travels up to the cloudy speck in the handle of Orion's sword, and bids it blaze forth into a galaxy as vast as ours, stands higher in the order of being than all that host of luminaries. The intellect of Newton which discovered the law that holds the revolving worlds together, is a nobler work of God than a universe of universes of unthinking matter.

If, still treading the loftiest paths of analogy, we adopt the supposition,—to me I own the grateful supposition,—that the countless planetary worlds which attend these countless suns, are the abodes of rational beings like man, instead of bringing back from this exalted conception a feeling of insignificance, as if the individuals of our race were but poor atoms in the infinity of being, I regard it, on the contrary, as a glory of our human nature, that it belongs to a family which no man can number of rational natures like itself. In the order of being they may stand beneath us, or they may stand above us; *he* may well be content with his place, who is made "a little lower than the angels."

[40]

CONTEMPLATION OF THE HEAVENS.

Finally, my Friends, I believe there is no contemplation better adapted to awaken devout ideas than that of the heavenly bodies,—no branch of natural science which bears clearer testimony to the power and wisdom of God than that to which you this day consecrate a temple. The heart of the ancient world, with all the prevailing ignorance of the true nature and motions of the heavenly orbs, was religiously impressed by their survey. There is a passage in one of those admirable philosophical treatises of Cicero composed in the decline of life, as a solace under domestic bereavement and patriotic concern at the impending convulsions of the state, in which, quoting from some lost work of Aristotle, he treats the topic in a manner which almost puts to shame the teachings of Christian wisdom.

"Præclare ergo Aristoteles, 'Si essent,' inquit, 'qui sub terra semper habitavissent, bonis et illustribus domiciliis quæ essent ornata signis atque picturis, instructaque rebus iis omnibus quibus abundant ii qui beati putantur, nec tamen exissent unquam supra terram; accepissent autem fama et auditione, esse quoddam numen et vim Deorum,—deinde aliquo tempore patefactis terræ faucibus ex illis abditis sedibus evadere in hæc loca quæ nos incolimus, atque exire potuissent; cum repente terram et maria coelumque, vidissent; nubium magnitudinem ventorumque vim, cognovissent; aspexissentque solem, ejusque tum magnitudinem, pulchritudinemque; tum etiam efficientiam cognovissent, quod is diem efficeret, toto cœlo luce diffusa; cum autem terras nox opacasset, tum cœlum totum cernerent astris distinctum et ornatum, lunæque luminum varietatem tum crescentis tum senescentis, corumque omnium ortus et occasus atque in æternitate ratos immutabilesque cursus;—hæc cum viderent, profecto et esse Deos, et hæc tanta opera Deorum esse, arbitrarentur."[A]

There is much by day to engage the attention of the Observatory; the sun, his apparent motions, his dimensions, the spots on his disc (to us the faint indications of movements of unimagined grandeur in his luminous atmosphere), a solar eclipse, a transit of the inferior planets, the mysteries of the spectrum;—all phenomena of vast importance and interest. But night is the astronomer's accepted time; he goes to his delightful labors when the [41]busy world goes to its rest. A dark pall spreads over the resorts of active life; terrestrial objects, hill and valley, and rock and stream, and the abodes of men disappear; but the curtain is drawn up which concealed the heaven-ly hosts. There they shine and there they move, as they moved and shone to the eyes of Newton and Galileo, of Kepler and Copernicus, of Ptolemy and Hipparchus; yes, as they moved and shone when the morning stars sang together, and all the sons of God shouted for joy. All has changed on earth; but the glorious heavens remain un-changed. The plow passes over the site of mighty cities, — the homes of powerful nations are desolate, the languages they spoke are for-gotten; but the stars that shone for them are shining for us; the same eclipses run their steady cycle; the same equinoxes call out the flow-ers of spring, and send the husbandman to the harvest; the sun pauses at either tropic as he did when his course began; and sun and moon, and planet and satellite, and star and constellation and galaxy, still bear witness to the power, the wisdom, and the love, which placed them in the heavens and uphold them there.

[A] "Nobly does Aristotle observe, that if there were beings who had always lived under ground, in convenient, nay, in magnificent dwellings, adorned with statues and pictures, and every thing which belongs to prosperous life, but who had never come above ground; who had heard, however, by fame and report, of the being and power of the gods; if, at a certain time, the portals of the earth being thrown open, they had been able to emerge from those hid-den abodes to the regions inhabited by us; when suddenly they had seen the earth, the sea, and the sky; had perceived the vastness of the clouds and the force of the winds; had contemplated the sun, his magnitude and his beauty, and still more his effectual power, that it is he who makes the day, by the diffusion of his light through the whole sky; and, when night had darkened the earth, should then behold the whole heavens studded and adorned with stars, and the various lights of the waxing and waning moon, the risings and the settings of all these heavenly bodies, and the courses fixed and im-mutable in all eternity; when, I say, they should see these things, truly they would believe that there were gods, and these so great things are their works." — Cicero, *De Natura Deorum* lib. ii., § 30.